# Leagues Apart

•ANDREW "RUBE" FOSTER•

# Leagues Apart

## The Men and Times of the Negro Baseball Leagues

Text by
**Lawrence S. Ritter**

Illustrations by
**Richard Merkin**

**Morrow Junior Books**

**New York**

*A special thanks to my friend Luis Muñoz*
*for sharing his profound knowledge of place and Caribbean baseball with me.*
*His assistance is always appreciated.*
—R.M.

Oil pastels were used for the full-color illustrations.
The text type is 14-point Guardi.

Printed in the United States of America.

1 2 3 4 5 6 7 8 9 10

Library of Congress Cataloging-in-Publication Data
Ritter, Lawrence S.
Leagues apart: the men and times of the Negro baseball leagues/
text by Lawrence S. Ritter; illustrations by Richard Merkin.
p.   cm.
ISBN 0-688-13316-9 (trade)—ISBN 0-688-13317-7 (library)
1. Negro leagues—History—Juvenile literature.   [1. Negro leagues—History.   2. Baseball—History.]
I. Merkin, Richard, ill.   II. Title.   GV875.A1R58 1995   796.357′64′0973—dc20   94-17512   CIP  AC

For Luke, Melissa, and Tara
*Con Amor*
—L.R.


For Robert Peterson, who gave us *Only the Ball Was White*—the
true Old Testament for those who love these great men and
the game that they played. And for my friend Max Manning,
who pitched for the Newark Eagles for seven years and
taught children for twenty-eight.
—R.M.

·GEORGE HERMAN "BABE" RUTH·

**W**ho is the greatest baseball player who ever lived?

That seems like an easy question, doesn't it? But it must be harder than it looks because even the experts can't seem to agree on the answer. For instance, many swear on a stack of Bibles that **George Herman Ruth** is the greatest of all time. Babe Ruth started as a pitcher, became one of the best in the game, and then gave it up and became a phenomenal home run slugger.

The Babe walloped 714 homers during his career. Since it is 360 feet around the bases, he trotted almost 50 miles rounding the bases after hitting the ball into the stands or clear out of the ballpark! (He also received 2,056 bases on balls, which is an additional 35 miles, but that's another story.)

**· HANK AARON AND WILLIE MAYS ·**

However, not everyone thinks the Babe should be ranked all-time number one. Instead, many would choose **Hank Aaron**, the man who broke Ruth's lifetime home run record. Aaron blasted 755 homers, 41 more than Ruth.

Still others say that the best baseball player ever was neither Babe Ruth nor Hank Aaron. They prefer **Willie Mays**, who was a remarkable fielder and baserunner as well as a marvelous hitter. Mays hit 660 home runs, which is fewer than Ruth or Aaron hit. But he was a better outfielder and stole over 300 bases, which is a lot more than Ruth or Aaron stole.

Something that most people, even most baseball fans, don't know about Henry Louis Aaron and Willie Howard Mays is that they both learned how to play the game from veteran Negro League ballplayers. That's because they both began their careers in the Negro Leagues.

The Negro Leagues . . . if the name isn't familiar or sounds old-fashioned, it's because, like dinosaurs, the Negro Leagues have been extinct for a long time; they faded away in the 1950s.

Before about 1950, if you were black and wanted to earn a living playing baseball, you were not allowed to play on the same team with white ballplayers. Prejudiced team owners, encouraged by bigoted players, established racist rules that prevented black athletes from playing in the major leagues, regardless of their skills.

Take **Smokey Joe Williams**, for example. The tall right-hander pitched from 1905 to 1932, mainly for the Chicago American Giants, the New York Lincoln Giants, and the Homestead Grays. He had a fastball that was said to zip in at well over 90 miles an hour, about as fast as that of the legendary Walter Johnson. Nevertheless, his name is unknown to most baseball fans because he was never permitted to wear a major league uniform.

·SMOKEY JOE WILLIAMS·

## ·CANNONBALL DICK REDDING·

Or take **Cannonball Dick Redding**, a hard-throwing righthander who pitched with a scary windup: Kicking high with his left leg, he would pivot on his right foot to face second base, showing the batter his back, then swing around and quickly fire the ball to the catcher. For a number of years he and Smokey Joe made the New York Lincoln Giants the most feared of all black teams.

· JAMES "COOL PAPA" BELL ·

Another example is **James "Cool Papa" Bell**, the swiftest outfielder and fastest runner in the Negro Leagues' history. He played from the early twenties into the forties. Bell specialized in infield singles, stretching doubles into triples, and stealing bases.

Black ballplayers had no choice in those days but to join poorly paid teams made up of black players like themselves. Some of these teams formed leagues—the two most important were the Negro National League and the Negro American League—and, like the major leagues, they played a long schedule of games. They had their own pennant races, all-star games, and often a world series between the two pennant winners.

The guiding light behind the Negro National League was **Andrew "Rube" Foster**, often called the Father of Black Baseball. An excellent pitcher, he also became the manager and owner of the Chicago American Giants. His greatest achievement, however, was organizing the Negro National League, in 1920.

Negro League teams included the Bacharach Giants of Atlantic City, the Birmingham Black Barons (where Willie Mays played), the Chicago American Giants, the Hilldale Club of Philadelphia, the Indianapolis Clowns (Hank Aaron's first team), the Kansas City Monarchs, the Newark Eagles, the New York Black Yankees, the New York Lincoln Giants, the Philadelphia Stars, the Pittsburgh Crawfords, and the Homestead Grays. The Grays had *two* homes: Pittsburgh, Pennsylvania, and Washington, D.C.

•ANDREW "RUBE" FOSTER•

Before passage of the civil rights laws in the 1960s, black Americans often had trouble finding hotels where they could sleep overnight or restaurants where they could sit down and eat. The great Cool Papa Bell once described what life in the Negro Leagues used to be like:

*In addition to our regular league games, we'd "barnstorm" a lot. That means we'd play exhibition games, in one city one day and in another city the next. We traveled in our own private bus, not by train or plane, and every night we'd have to find a place to stay if we weren't*

in a big city up North. Often no hotel would have us—they were for whites only—and we'd have to stay in rooming houses or with private families, colored families, a few of us in each house.

We went into a lot of small towns where we couldn't find any place to sleep, so we slept on the bus. If we had to, we could convert the seats into beds. We'd pull over to the side of the road, in a cornfield or someplace, and sleep until the break of day, and then we'd go on into the next town, hoping we could find a restaurant that would be willing to serve us. Things like that, today people wouldn't believe it.

**·MARTIN DIHIGO·**

In the 1920s and 1930s some ballplayers protested against discrimination in the game—Yankee first baseman Lou Gehrig, for one—but it didn't do any good.

Although African American ballplayers were discriminated against in the United States, they were warmly welcomed in many baseball-loving Latin American countries—especially in Mexico, Panama, Venezuela, and the Caribbean islands (Cuba, the Dominican Republic, and Puerto Rico). There they played on integrated teams and did not have to face racial hostility.

Some ballplayers were special favorites in Latin America. One of them was **Martín Dihigo**. Born in Cuba in 1905, Dihigo was a star pitcher who also played infield or outfield and was a terrific hitter. Many old-timers claim he was the greatest all-around player who ever lived. Not surprisingly, he was a national hero in Cuba.

## ·JOHN HENRY "POP" LLOYD·

    Another player, shortstop **John Henry "Pop" Lloyd**, was idolized in Mexico. A six-footer, which is rather tall for a shortstop, he was a sensational fielder and a career .340 hitter from 1905 to 1931. Veteran players say there has never been a better all-around shortstop.

The two best-known Negro Leaguers were pitcher Satchel Paige and catcher Josh Gibson. Everyone agrees that if they had played in the majors, both would have become superstars.

**LeRoy "Satchel" Paige** was six feet three and 175 pounds soaking wet. He threw and batted righthanded. Paige is usually ranked as the greatest black pitcher—many say *the* greatest pitcher, black or white—of all time. By the time racial segregation in baseball ended, in 1947, Satchel was already forty-one years old. Even so, the Cleveland Indians signed him on July 7, 1948, his forty-second birthday.

Despite his age, Satchel Paige pitched in the major leagues until 1953. In 1952 he won twelve games, including two shutouts, and saved ten more in relief for a next-to-last-place team. And in 1965, to cap it all off, Paige pitched three scoreless innings for Kansas City against the Boston Red Sox and allowed only one hit. He was fifty-nine years old then and remains the oldest player ever to have participated in a major league game.

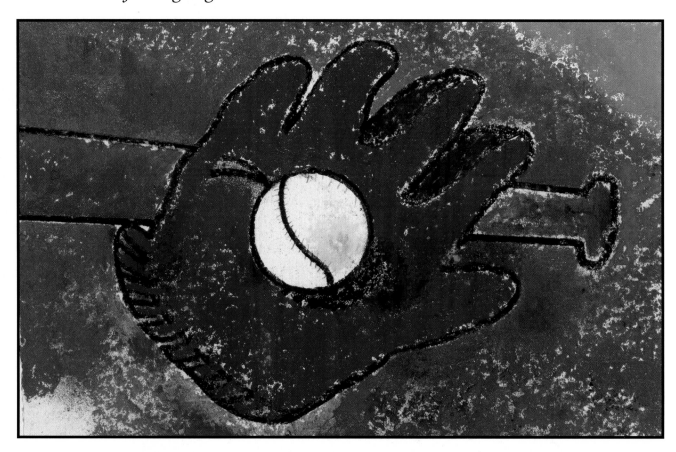

·LEROY "SATCHEL" PAIGE·

•JOSH GIBSON•

Catcher **Josh Gibson** did not fare as well. The big right-handed slugger played most of his career with the Homestead Grays. Although the Negro Leagues had a number of great home run hitters, the powerfully built, genial, moon-faced Gibson, whom many called the black Babe Ruth, was the greatest of all. By the time segregation ended, Josh Gibson was dead. He died of a stroke early in 1947, at the age of thirty-five.

Paige and Gibson were the best-known Negro League players, but they were not the only outstanding ones. Three other great pitchers, for example, were Bullet Joe Rogan, Willie Foster, and Jose Mendez.

**· WILBUR "BULLET JOE" ROGAN ·**

**Wilbur "Bullet Joe" Rogan** was one of the most versatile players in baseball history. He not only pitched but also batted cleanup for the Kansas City Monarchs during the twenties and early thirties. The Bullet, a righthander, was in the same class as Babe Ruth and Martin Dihigo when it came to the ability to excel in just about every aspect of the game.

·WILLIE FOSTER·

**Willie Foster** was probably the best lefthanded pitcher in the history of the Negro Leagues. Rube Foster's kid brother pitched brilliantly from the early twenties to the late thirties, mainly for Rube's Chicago American Giants.

Cuban-born **Jose Mendez**, a righthanded fastball pitcher, regularly defeated major league teams visiting Cuba. He also played several infield positions, but he was famous mostly because of his great skill as a pitcher. As a manager, Mendez led the Kansas City Monarchs to three Negro National League pennants.

JOSE MENDEZ

·LOUIS SANTOP·

Josh Gibson wasn't the only home run slugger in the Negro Leagues. He had plenty of competition.

Catcher **Louis Santop** was the first of the great Negro League power hitters. The burly six-foot-three 230-pounder, a lefthanded batter and righthanded thrower, smashed towering Babe Ruth–type homers that carried great distances. Like the Babe, he was a huge gate attraction.

**George "Mule" Suttles** played first base from the twenties to the forties for the Birmingham Black Barons and other teams. Righthanded at bat and in the field, Mule hit booming home runs that made him extremely popular with the fans, who delighted in chanting, *"Kick,* Mule, *kick,"* whenever he stepped into the batter's box.

Outfielder Norman "Turkey" Stearnes, a lefthander, was a remarkable long-ball hitter despite his slender build. Loved by the fans for his numerous home runs, he was chosen for four of the first five all-star teams (in 1933, 1934, 1935, and 1937), even though by then he was well past his peak.

· GEORGE "MULE" SUTTLES ·

· CRISTOBAL TORRIENTE ·

Oscar Charleston is the greatest all-around outfielder in the Negro Leagues' history. The barrel-chested lefthander played for the Chicago American Giants and the Pittsburgh Crawfords. He was a league-leading hitter, a whirlwind on the bases, a circus-catch outfielder, and a fine first baseman as well. He was often called the black Ty Cobb, but many thought Ty Cobb should really be called the white Oscar Charleston.

Outfielder **Cristobal Torriente** packed 190 pounds of muscle on a stocky five-foot-ten frame. Born in Cuba in 1895, the lefthander was a line-drive home run slugger who also hit for a high batting average. Torriente starred with the Chicago American Giants and with teams in Latin America, especially in his native Cuba.

**·WALTER "BUCK" LEONARD·**

    Many skillful infielders snared line drives while in Negro League uniforms. Take first baseman **Walter "Buck" Leonard**, for instance, who was often called the black Lou Gehrig. With Buck playing first base, the Homestead Grays won nine pennants.

**Willie "Devil" Wells** was Pop Lloyd's chief rival as the Negro Leagues' greatest shortstop. He had a lengthy career, from 1923 to 1949, mainly with the St. Louis Stars, Chicago American Giants, Newark Eagles, and teams in Mexico and the Caribbean. Wells got his nickname because of the many ingenious (and devilish) ways he figured out to beat opponents with his clutch hitting, acrobatic fielding, and quick thinking.

·WILLIE "DEVIL" WELLS·

## · WILLIAM "JUDY" JOHNSON ·

**William "Judy" Johnson** is most often chosen as one of the two best third basemen in the Negro Leagues' history. He played with Philadelphia's Hilldale Club in the twenties and with the Pittsburgh Crawfords in the thirties. The thin third baseman was known for his line drive clutch hitting and dazzling fielding.

Ray "Squatty" (also known as "Hooks") Dandridge is Judy Johnson's chief rival as the greatest third baseman in the Negro Leagues' history. A bowlegged 175-pound spark plug, Ray starred with the Newark Eagles in the thirties and then played mostly in Mexico and Cuba in the forties. He was signed by Minneapolis in the newly integrated American Association in 1949, and in 1950 was voted, at age thirty-seven, that league's most valuable player.

Segregation in baseball started to crumble in 1942, when Branch Rickey became president of the Brooklyn Dodgers. In 1945, when World War II ended, Rickey decided that he would no longer honor the unwritten agreement that banned African Americans from the major leagues.

The man Rickey chose to blaze the trail and desegregate the game was **Jackie Robinson**, then a shortstop for the Kansas City Monarchs. Jack Roosevelt Robinson had been a baseball, football, basketball, *and* track star at UCLA, the University of California at Los Angeles. Signed by Rickey late in 1945, Robinson was sent in 1946 to Montreal, Canada, where Brooklyn had a farm club in the International League, until then an all-white league. That year he led Montreal to a pennant while also leading the league in batting!

On Tuesday, April 15, 1947, at two o'clock in the afternoon, a broad-shouldered Jackie Robinson, wearing a Brooklyn uniform, sprang out of the home team's dugout at Ebbets Field to take his position at first base. He was the first black player in the major leagues.

JACKIE ROBINSON

As soon as it was known that Jackie was a Dodger, four of his teammates asked to be traded. During games a barrage of racial insults was directed at him from fans in the stands and from the opposing team's bench. Some players said they would go on strike rather than play with or against a black man.

National League President Ford Frick responded with a blunt ultimatum. "I do not care if half the league strikes," he said. "Those who do will be suspended and I don't care if it wrecks the league for five years. This is the United States of America, and one citizen has as much right to play as another."

This angry statement—which should have been made by someone in authority about fifty years earlier—had such a sobering effect that resistance quickly collapsed.

In his first season with the Dodgers Robinson led the National League in stolen bases and was voted rookie of the year. In 1949 he led the league in hitting and was named its most valuable player. It has been said that Rickey signed Jackie Robinson not for idealistic reasons but because he wanted to win ball games. If so, Rickey knew what he was doing, because Brooklyn won six pennants in the ten years Jackie was there.

**·MONTE IRVIN·**

With Robinson's success, other Negro Leaguers were pursued by major league teams. Roy Campanella of the Baltimore Elite Giants joined the Brooklyn (now the Los Angeles) Dodgers in 1948, and **Monte Irvin** of the Newark Eagles reported to the New York (now the San Francisco) Giants in 1949. Ernie Banks of the Kansas City Monarchs signed with the Chicago Cubs in 1953, and the New York Yankees acquired their first black player in 1955—catcher Elston Howard, also of the Monarchs.

As might have been expected, integration meant the end of
the trail for the Negro Leagues. Since black and white could
now play on the same teams and in the same leagues, the
Negro Leagues' fundamental reason for existing disappeared.
In addition, African American baseball fans abandoned
the Negro League teams and flocked instead to major league

ballparks to see Jackie and Satchel and the others play with and against established major league stars.

The Negro National League got the message right away and shut down at the end of the 1948 season. The Negro American League struggled through the fifties with fewer and fewer teams and then disbanded as well.

And how did former Negro Leaguers do when they got their long-awaited chance in the majors? Not too poorly, thank you: In the dozen years from 1949 through 1960, they won two major league batting crowns, seven runs batted in titles, eight home run crowns, and nine most valuable player awards!

Thus ended an ugly and shameful chapter in American history. When we look back, it is tempting to view the past through rose-colored glasses and glamorize the Negro League experience: busloads of carefree ballplayers barnstorming happily across the land, playing America's national pastime in cities and towns large and small.

But these talented men were not in the Negro Leagues by choice. They were there because of high walls erected in the name of segregation and maintained by racism. Poorly paid and neglected, they were there because they were not allowed to compete against their equals, the Ruths, Gehrigs, and DiMaggios, who were well paid and showered with fame and prestige.

It may be too late to compensate these fine athletes for what they lost through no fault of their own, but the least we can do is remember their names and honor their memories.

Hard-hitting outfielder Gene Benson, who played in the thirties and forties with the Bacharach Giants and Philadelphia Stars, summed up the bittersweet feelings of many Negro Leaguers in a conversation with writer John Holway. "We never thought about the major leagues," Benson said. "We never dreamed that it would come true. But I know we were the pioneers. Without our league, where would Robinson have come from? If we weren't out there suffering and struggling, they wouldn't have any blacks in there now."

African American ballplayers have been outstanding batters, fielders, and pitchers in the major leagues since Jackie Robinson demolished the color barrier in 1947. Their performance since then demonstrates what they could have done in earlier years.

So when we think about the Honor Roll of Great Ballplayers, like Babe Ruth and Mickey Mantle and Hank Aaron, let's not forget the wonderful Negro Leaguers, like Josh and Cool Papa, Cannonball Dick and Bullet Joe, and all the others who never got a chance to show their stuff in the major leagues.

# HALL OF FAMERS

The following men, who spent all or most of their careers in the Negro Leagues, have been elected to the Baseball Hall of Fame at Cooperstown. The year each was elected is in parentheses.

**LeRoy "Satchel" Paige (1971)**

**Josh Gibson (1972)**

**Walter "Buck" Leonard (1972)**

**Monte Irvin (1973)**

**James "Cool Papa" Bell (1974)**

**William "Judy" Johnson (1975)**

**Oscar Charleston (1976)**

**Martin Dihigo (1977)**

**John Henry "Pop" Lloyd (1977)**

**Andrew "Rube" Foster (1981)**

**Ray "Squatty" Dandridge (1987)**